The Berenstain Bears. SUMMER FUN!

Includes:

The Berenstain Bears GO TO CAMP

The Berenstain Bears GO OUT FOR THE TEAM

The Berenstain Bears GET THEIR KICKS

Stan & Jan Berenst[ain]

RANDOM HOUSE 🏠 NEW YORK

Copyright © 1982, 1986, 1998, 2020 by Berenstain Enterprises, Inc.
All rights reserved.
Published in the United States by Random House Children's Books, a division of
Penguin Random House LLC, 1745 Broadway, New York, NY 10019, and in Canada by
Penguin Random House Canada Limited, Toronto. Originally published in different form by
Random House Children's Books, New York, as *The Berenstain Bears Go to Camp* in 1982,
The Berenstain Bears Go Out for the Team in 1986, and *The Berenstain Bears Get Their Kicks* in 1998.

Random House and the colophon are registered trademarks of Penguin Random House LLC.

Visit us on the Web!
rhcbooks.com
BerenstainBears.com

Library of Congress Control Number: 2019951237
ISBN 978-0-593-17611-5

MANUFACTURED IN CHINA
10 9 8 7 6 5 4 3 2 1

The Berenstain Bears
GO TO CAMP

It was the last day of school and the beginning of vacation—that wonderful time when little bears could sit around doing absolutely nothing. Brother Bear and Sister Bear shouted good-bye to Teacher Jane and hopped onto the bus for the happy trip home.

"Well?" asked Mama Bear after a day or so of vacation. "Are you enjoying sitting around doing nothing?"
"It's great!" said Sister.
"Absolutely!" said Brother.
"There's just one trouble with it," added Sister. *"There's nothing to do!"*

"Here, take a look at this," said Mama
as she reached for something that had
come in the mail.

This is what it looked like:

TIRED OF SITTING AROUND DOING NOTHING? COME TO GRIZZLY BOB'S DAY CAMP SUMMER FUN FOR CUBS OF ALL AGES

Some of the things looked interesting. But Brother wondered what "fully supervised" meant. And Sister wasn't so sure about that "overnight sleep-out." It sounded a little scary.

"Where is this camp?" asked Sister.

"Not far," answered Mama.

"How will we get there?" Brother wanted to know.

"A bus comes for you in the morning and brings you home in the afternoon."

"Sounds a little like school," said Brother.

"We'll think about it," said the cubs, and went back to doing nothing—well, not exactly nothing. . . .

They picked a few wildflowers,

chased a few butterflies,

turned over a few rocks . . .

—and thought about it.

"Mama, could we try Grizzly Bob's Day Camp just to see if we like it?" they asked.

"Of course," said Mama.

A couple of mornings later, Brother and Sister
were in camp shorts and T-shirts,
all ready and waiting when the bus came.

It didn't look much like
the school bus.

And Grizzly Bob
didn't look much like Teacher Jane.

And the camp didn't look
anything like school!

Grizzly Bob had built his camp beside a lake at the edge of the forest. There were log buildings, a flagpole flying the camp flag, a big bulletin board with the camp rules—there certainly were a lot of rules—some interesting paths, a roped-in place to swim. . . . There was even a big red canoe!

Bob had made name tags for the cubs. "You're campmates now, so you better get to know each other," he said.

Then he took them on a tour of the camp. There was an office with a desk, where he did his paperwork, and a first-aid corner full of bandages and things for cuts and bruises.

There was a Rec Hall to go into when it rained. "Rec" was short for recreation.

There was a picnic place and a barbecue pit where they roasted hot dogs for lunch. Sister burned hers a little, but she traded with another cub who liked burned hot dogs.

Bob announced that after lunch they would all climb up Spook Hill to the very top of Skull Rock—the special place where they would have their end-of-camp powwow and sleep-out.

It was quite a climb!

That evening Mama and Papa Bear were eager to know how the cubs liked camp.

"It was okay," said Brother. "But they sure have a lot of rules!"

"It was all right," agreed Sister. "They sure have plenty of bandages and stingy stuff for cuts!"

But what they were both thinking about was Skull Rock and that end-of-camp sleep-out.

Especially Sister.

The second day was different. Brother had a great day. He passed the swimming test and was allowed to ride in the canoe.

Sister didn't have such a good day. She played dodge ball and some of the cubs threw pretty hard.

The third day Sister had fun. She got a star for a birch picture frame she made in arts and crafts. But Brother hurt his knee in the wheelbarrow race.

The fourth day both
of them had fun—

And every day after that! So
much fun that they forgot
about Skull Rock and
the sleep-out . . .

—almost.

Papa found the sleeping bags that he and Mama had used on their honeymoon, and when the camp bus came on the morning of the big night, Brother and Sister were ready . . . sort of.

The climb up Spook Hill wasn't so hard this time—even with backpacks. The cubs were strong and tough from their summer of camping. Tomorrow would be Field Day—the last day of camp, when their parents would come to watch their games and contests and see awards given out. But, for now, all the cubs could think about was the big sleep-out.

It was just beginning to
get dark when they reached
Skull Rock.

Grizzly Bob built a campfire. Then he went into a small cave. When he came out, he was dressed in a beautiful Indian costume!

Then the cubs sat in a semicircle, and the powwow began.

Bob told them old Indian legends of
the great animal spirits—the story
of the Great Grizzly as Big as a
Mountain, the Soaring Eagle Who Filled
the Sky, and the Mighty Salmon Whose
Colors Made the Rainbow.

As Bob told the old stories, the cubs could almost see the wonderful creatures in the firelit smoke as it curled up into the night sky.

After the powwow, they had cocoa and honey bread. Then they curled up in their sleeping bags. And soon they were all fast asleep . . . even Sister.

The next day Brother and Sister did very well in the Field Day games and contests.

Brother won a trophy for finishing second in the dash, and Sister got medals for the dead-bear's float and for her bead belt.

It was almost the end of summer; school would be starting in a couple of weeks.

"Well?" asked Papa. "How did you like camp?"

"It was great!" said Brother, hugging his trophy.

"It was great!" agreed Sister, wearing her medals proudly. "But you know something? After Grizzly Bob's Day Camp, school will be like a vacation!"

The Berenstain Bears
GO OUT FOR THE TEAM

CHAMP

When little bears first
Show a will to compete,
It's hard for parents not to
Jump in with both feet.

Brother and Sister Bear, who lived with their mama and papa in the big tree house down a sunny dirt road deep in Bear Country, enjoyed the changing seasons—and the sports that went with them:

football and soccer in the fall...

basketball and
ice hockey in the
winter . . .

and their favorite,
baseball in the spring.

As soon as Brother and Sister felt the first warmth of the spring sun, they got out their trusty ball, bat, and gloves and began limbering up for the season.

They played pitch-and-catch...
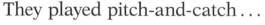

and practiced batting.

Why, they even studied up on the rules of the game.

Pretty soon some of their friends came to join in the baseball fun.

After a while Brother looked around and said, "Hey, I think we have enough for a game. Let's go over to Farmer Ben's back meadow and choose up sides."

Farmer Ben was a good neighbor. He had been allowing cubs to play baseball in his meadow for years. Of course, the grassy meadow wasn't a real baseball field, so there were a few problems and some special ground rules.

There were no foul lines, just base paths worn by year after year of cubs running the bases. So there were a lot of arguments about foul balls. There was a rule against sliding into second base, because second base was a rock. And any ball that was hit into the duck pond in left field was a ground-rule double and an automatic time-out while they fished it out.

But arguments, rocks, and duck ponds
didn't worry Brother, Sister, and
their friends. They chose up sides
and started a game.

Sister had done some growing since last season, and when she went to bat she whacked her very first ground-rule double. All the cubs—and even the ducks—were surprised.

And her knowledge of the rules came in handy when Cousin Freddie forgot to touch second base on his way to third. She called for the ball, tagged second, and declared him out. He made a big fuss, but she pointed out that those were the rules.

"Isn't that right?" she asked Farmer Ben, who was watching from the sideline.

"Right as rain," said Farmer Ben.

The game moved right along until
Brother hit a ball all the way into
the next field and Farmer Ben's
goat got it.

"Back so soon?" asked Papa, looking up from his paper as Brother and Sister trooped back home.

"Yep!" said Sister, holding up the ball. "Game called off on account of Farmer Ben's goat chewing the cover off the ball."

Papa was pretty impressed when he heard about Brother's hit and Sister's ground-rule double.

"Seems to me," said Papa, "that you cubs might want to think about playing some real baseball on a real baseball field. It says right here in the paper that the Bear Country Cub League is going to be holding tryouts pretty soon. You might want to sign up."

"Now, hold on," interrupted Mama. "That's a high-powered league over there, and those tryouts involve quite a lot of pressure."

"Pressure?" asked Sister. "What do you mean?"

"You'll be competing against lots of other cubs and not everybody is going to make the team," said Mama. "But you both play pretty well," she added, "so it's up to you."

"Won't hurt to drive over and have a look," said Papa.

"Wow!" said Brother when he saw the Cub
League field. It was a real field with fences
and foul lines and real bases and grandstands
and everything.

And the teams wore uniforms!
Brother and Sister signed up
right then and there!

BEAR COUNTRY CUB LEAGUE

LAST YEAR'S
CHAMPS

SIGN
UP
HERE

They got ready for the tryouts by practicing. They practiced fielding and hitting. Mama showed them how to choke up on the bat against fast pitching. They even practiced bunting and base running. But as tryout day drew near, they began to get a little nervous.

"Try to calm down," said Mama. "It's only a game. Besides, the worst that can happen is that you won't make the team. You can always try out again next year."

"No, that's not the worst that can happen," said Brother, looking gloomy. "The worst that can happen is if Sis makes the team and *I don't*!"

"I consider that a sexist remark!" snapped Sister angrily.

"Well, not completely," said Mama. "After all, Brother's older than you and he's very proud of his baseball ability."

"I see what you mean about pressure," said Sister.

Finally the day of the tryouts came. There were cubs all over the field—and league officials with clipboards and sunglasses so you couldn't see what they were thinking. Each cub had a number, and the officials moved around the field watching the cubs and making checks on their clipboards. Talk about pressure!

Brother and Sister were nervous at first. Sister missed an easy ground ball and Brother swung too hard at bat, missed the ball completely, and fell down on the seat of his pants. But as the tryouts continued, they both settled down and did a little better.

Brother remembered to choke up on the bat. He hit a good single and went to second base when the fielder bobbled the ball. Sister fielded some grounders well, and once when she was batting, the catcher dropped the third strike and she ran to first base even though she had struck out. There was a big fuss, but an official was watching and said she was right.

"Well, how did you do?" asked Mama when she and Papa came to pick the cubs up after the tryouts.

"Hard to say," answered Brother. "We certainly weren't the best."

"But we weren't the worst, either," said Sister. "Anyway—it's only a game and the worst that can happen is that we won't make the team."

"Yeah," sighed Brother. "We can always try again next year if we want to."

"When will you know?" asked Papa as they headed home.

"They're going to post the results on the bulletin board tomorrow," said Brother.

"Well," said Papa the next day, "don't you think we ought to drive over and check up?"
"I guess so," said Brother.
"May as well," said Sister.

When they reached the field, Brother and Sister ran to the bulletin board.

"Talk about pressure," said
Papa, mopping his brow as he
and Mama waited in the car.
"Indeed," said Mama, fanning
herself.

At last Mama and Papa heard a shout as Brother and Sister burst out of the crowd around the bulletin board.

"We made it! We made it!" they shouted, jumping for joy.

"There are four teams in the league!" shouted Sister. "The Cardinals, the Bluejays, the Orioles, and the Catbirds! We both made the Cardinals!"

"Terrific!" said Papa.

"Congratulations!" said Mama.

On the day of the first game, the cubs looked elegant in their uniforms, and Mama and Papa sat up front in the grandstand. Brother was up to bat against the Bluejays. The pitcher wound up and threw a fastball. Brother watched it go by.

"Strike one!" called the umpire.

"That was no strike!" screamed Mama, waving her hat. "It was wide by a mile! Call yourself an umpire!"

"Mama, please!" hissed Sister from the sideline. "Calm down! And remember— it's only a game!"

"Sorry about that," said Mama. Then she straightened her hat, sat down, and enjoyed the rest of the game.

The Berenstain Bears
GET THEIR
KICKS

All soccer moms know
it's a new game, Bub,
when a big ol' papa bear
can learn from his cub.

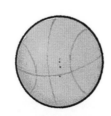

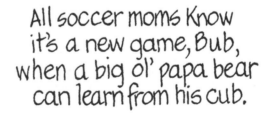

Papa Bear's family, friends, and neighbors all knew that he was a "traditional" sort of fellow. That means he liked to do the things he'd always done in pretty much the same ways he'd always done them. He liked to use traditional tools in his work as a woodsbear— though he did use more modern tools when he absolutely had to.

He was a shirt-and-overalls kind of guy when it came to clothes. He was a meat-and-potatoes kind of guy when it came to food. And when it came to sports, Papa was devoted to the games he'd grown up with: football in the fall, basketball in the winter, and in the summer, baseball, of course.

Papa loved baseball:

the smack of the ball
in the catcher's mitt,

the pull on the shoulders
after that first hard swing,

THWOCK

the loud *"thwock!"* of the ball
on the bat when you hit a high
fly over the fielder's head.

So when cubs Brother and Sister fell head over heels in love with soccer, Papa Bear got a little upset—especially when it turned out that Mama, who had played soccer as a cub, had signed up to coach for the neighborhood league.

So it was that on a bright sunny summer day, Papa bounded out of the tree house with a bat, a ball, and three gloves: a catcher's mitt for himself and two fielder's gloves for Brother and Sister.

"Get ready for some baseball!" he shouted.

"We'll shag some flies, work on the curve, and field some grounders!"

"Er, maybe some other time, Papa," said Brother. "But we're going to be busy today."

"Busy doing what?" asked Papa.

"Playing soccer," said Brother.

"Soccer?" said Papa. "You mean that game they play with that funny black-and-white ball?" Papa could hardly believe his ears. "Do you mean you'd rather play soccer than *baseball*?"

"Maybe we can play baseball later this afternoon," said Brother. "But soccer tryouts are today, and we have to get over to the soccer field for some early practice."

"That's right," said Sister. "I'm going to try out for the Kewpies."

"That's the younger team," said Brother. "I'm going to try out for the Buddies."

"The Kewpies? The Buddies?" said Papa. "What kind of team names are they? What's wrong with good old-fashioned baseball team names like Tigers, Sluggers, and Giants? Besides, I don't see why you have to practice. All you have to do is run around and kick that silly black-and-white ball once in a while."

"There's a lot more to soccer than that," said Mama. She had just come out of the house. It said "Soccer Mom" on her shirt.

"Like what?" asked Papa.

"Like all sorts of stuff," said Brother. "Like dribbling, passing, trapping, and headers."

"And all different kinds of kicks," added Sister.

"Humph!" humphed Papa. "I've never played soccer in my life," he said. "But I'll bet I can kick that silly ball farther and straighter than all three of you put together. Here, gimme that ball!"

Papa put the ball on the ground, stepped back a long way, and said, "See those two birch trees way over there?" The two birch trees were quite far away.

Then Papa charged forward at full speed. But he misjudged his kick, missed the ball completely, and landed on the ground with a mighty *"Oof!"*

OOF!

Mama and the cubs ran to Papa.

"Are you all right, dear?" said Mama as she and the cubs helped Papa get up.

"Of course I'm all right," said Papa. "Just let me try that again."

"Sorry, my dear," said Mama, picking up the ball. "But we must be on our way. Come along, cubs."

Papa watched as "Soccer Mom" Mama and the cubs headed for the soccer field, dribbling and passing as they went.

"Farther and straighter than all three of them put together," said Papa as he stared at a large stone that lay on the ground. "I'll show 'em!" he snarled, and he kicked the stone with all his might.

But it wasn't a stone at all. It was the top of a big buried rock.
"Y-E-E-E-O-W-W-W!" cried Papa as he hopped around holding his foot.

As Papa sat on a low stump rubbing his foot, he heard sounds coming from the soccer field, which lay just over the hill. "Maybe there's more to soccer than I thought," he said. "I think I'll go have a look." He limped off in the direction of the noise.

When Papa arrived at the field, he saw that there was, indeed, more to soccer than he'd thought—a lot more! There were cubs and coaches all over the field practicing. There were league officials moving among them, writing things down on clipboards.

Brother and Sister were right at the center of the action, learning different moves along with all the other cubs. They were learning:

SLOW IT DOWN EASY.

the trap,

KEEP IT CLOSE TO YOUR FEET.

the dribble,

KEEP YOUR EYE ON THE BALL.

the pass,

the instep kick,

FOLLOW THROUGH WITH YOUR FOOT.

KICK IT BEFORE IT HITS THE GROUND.

the volley,

and, of course, the header.

And who was teaching the header but "Soccer Mom" Mama herself.

And what's more, they had to do all those things without touching the ball with their hands! Baseball-loving Papa couldn't help being impressed.

SOCCER MOM

The cubs and Mama were so busy with their dribbles, kicks, and headers that they didn't see Papa. But Papa saw them, and he was rooting hard for his cubs to make their teams.

He also saw the league officials hand their reports to a bear who was wearing a sweatshirt that said "Commissioner."

Papa sidled over to the commissioner, who was studying the reports. "Er, sir," said Papa. "Have Sister and Brother Bear made their teams? I'm their dad."

"As a matter of fact, they have," said the commissioner. "Sister made the Kewpies and Brother made the Buddies. Now, if you'll excuse me, I'm just about to post the results."

"How about that!" said Papa with a big grin. He felt so good that he forgot all about his sore foot as he hurried home.

"Say," said Brother as they headed over to see the tryout results. "Isn't that Papa?"

"Hmm," thought Brother and Sister and Mama as they watched Papa head for home.

Brother and Sister were very happy to have made their teams. But they hadn't forgotten their promise to play a little baseball with Papa. They got the ball, bat, and gloves.

"How about a little baseball, Papa?" said Brother. "Here, catch!" he cried as he tossed the ball to Papa. But Papa didn't catch it. He gave it a header instead.

BOP!

It was a good thing he was wearing his soft brown hat or he might have gotten himself a big headache. As it was, it knocked him down.

The cubs and Mama ran over to him. "Papa! Papa!" cried Brother. "Why did you do that?"

"Oh, I just wanted to show you that if soccer is good enough for my cubs, it's good enough for me. I'll tell you what. Instead of playing a little baseball, why don't you two show me some of your best soccer moves?"

And Brother and Sister did—
while "Soccer Mom" Mama
and "Soccer Dad" Papa
watched proudly.